Enchanting Legacy
Unravelling the History of the Tuatha Dé Danann

By
Steve McCarten

Copyright © 2023 Steve McCarten
All rights reserved.
ISBN: 9798394932731

DEDICATION

To my dear children,

This book, Enchanting Legacy: Unravelling the History of the Tuatha Dé Danann is dedicated to you with all my love and admiration. As your parent, I want to impart to you a deep appreciation of our Irish heritage and a sense of wonder for the stories that have been passed down through the generations.

Through these pages, I hope you will be transported to a world of ancient gods and goddesses, heroes and heroines, and magical creaturesthat once roamed the land of our ancestors. I want you to know that these stories are a part of our identity, and they have shaped our cultureand traditions.

I hope that this book will ignite your curiosity and inspire you to explore the rich history of Ireland, to ask questions, and to seek out new knowledge. May it serve as a reminder that our past is a treasure tobe cherished and preserved for future generations.

With all my love,

Dad. X

Acknowledgments

For my wife Laura,
May your heart be filled with joy and laughter,
May your days be blessed with love and peace,
May your spirit be strong and unbreakable,
And may all your dreams and aspirations come to fruition.
May you always know that you are cherished and loved,
And may our lives be forever intertwined.

Irish Prayer – Unknown

Table of Contents

INTRODUCTION	6
Origins in Ancient Ireland	10
Arrival of the Divine Tribe	13
Divine Attributes and Enigmatic Powers	16
The Tuatha Dé Danann's Immortal Presence in Irish Mythology	18
Battles and Conquests of the Divine Race	21
Bridging Realms: Divine Encounters and Mortal Alliances	24
The Fading Echoes of the Tuatha Dé Danann	27
The Legacy of the Tuatha Dé Danann in Modern Times	30
Epilogue	33
ABOUT THE AUTHOR	35

INTRODUCTION

In the deep folds of Irish mythology, there exists a race of ethereal beings whose story weaves through the tapestry of ancient lands and echoes in the whispers of the wind. The Tuatha Dé Danann, a captivating and enigmatic race, holds a place of reverence in the hearts of those who have heard the tales passed down through the ages. Their origins, triumphs, and decline are shrouded in the mists of time, carrying with them an aura of mystique and wonder.

It is within these pages that we embark on a journey of discovery, guided by ancient texts, the remnants of folklore, and the whispers of those who have encountered the remnants of this divine race. "Enchanting Legacy: Unravelling the History of the Tuatha Dé Danann" invites you to step into a realm where battles are waged with both sword and sorcery, where magic intertwines with the mortal realm, and where the touch of the divine leaves an indelible mark on the land.

The origins of the Tuatha Dé Danann are veiled in legend and myth, drawing upon ancient tales of their arrival in Ireland. Some say they descended from the heavens on wings of silver, alighting upon the sacred soil with grace and beauty that enchanted all who beheld them. Others whisper of a great voyage across treacherous seas, guided by the shimmering light of the moon, until their journey brought them to the shores of the Emerald Isle. These stories, passed down through generations, hint at a race of beings beyond mortal comprehension, with a connection to the land that runs deeper than mere myth.

Once settled in Ireland, the Tuatha Dé Danann established themselves as divine rulers, their power unmatched and their wisdom revered. Theirs was a kingdom where magic and mortal coexisted, where the boundaries between the worlds blurred, and where the touch of the divine breathed life into the realm. The sacred hill of Tara became their capital, a place where the threads of mortal and divine fate intertwined, and where the voices of both realms found harmony.

Throughout their existence, the Tuatha Dé Danann shaped the course of Irish mythology, leaving an indelible mark upon the landscape of tales and legends. Their interactions with mortals became the stuff of folklore, with tales of divine guidance and intervention echoing through the annals of time.

Bards and poets sought their favour, invoking their names in verse and song, forever immortalizing the deeds of the divine race.

But with the passage of centuries, change swept across the land. New beliefs and cultural influences took hold, eclipsing the once-prominent position of the Tuatha Dé Danann. The rise of Christianity brought with it a shifting worldview, and the divine tribe found themselves gradually receding from the forefront of mortal consciousness. Yet, their essence could not be extinguished. Instead, it transformed, merging with the narratives of saints and Christian figures, melding their ancient mythos with the evolving tapestry of faith.

As the mists of time unfurled, the Tuatha Dé Danann found solace in the embrace of the Otherworld, retreating into the realms of the Sidhe, the fairy folk of Irish mythology. Legends tell of the elusive encounters with these ethereal beings, the whispers in the wind that still carry the echoes of their presence. Their retreat marked not an end, but a transformation, as they became beings of mystery and enchantment, dwelling in the hidden places where mortal eyes seldom tread.

Today, the legacy of the Tuatha Dé Danann lives on, woven into the very fabric of Irish culture and identity. Their stories continue to captivate the hearts and minds of those who embrace the mythical and the fantastical. From the realms of literature to the realms of art and music, their presence can be felt in the creative expressions that seek to capture their ethereal essence.

In the realm of literature, the tales of the Tuatha Dé Danann inspire authors to delve into the depths of their mythology, spinning new narratives that breathe life into ancient characters. Writers, like sorcerers wielding pens, conjure vivid worlds where the divine race walks once more, their magical abilities and complex personalities captivating readers with every page turned. Their stories transcend time, transcending the boundaries of reality, and immersing readers in a world both familiar and wondrously strange.

Art, too, becomes a canvas upon which the Tuatha Dé Danann's legacy unfolds. Painters and sculptors, their hands guided by inspiration, craft images that evoke the beauty and power of these divine beings. Their ethereal features come alive on canvas, their radiant presence captured in strokes of paint and chisel marks. The artistry reflects the enduring allure of the Tuatha Dé Danann, inviting viewers to peer into a realm where mortal and divine intertwine.

Music, the language of the soul, weaves the melodies that resonate with the echoes of the divine. Composers draw from the wellspring of Tuatha Dé Danann's mythology, infusing their compositions with the essence of their legends. The haunting melodies evoke the mysteries of the Otherworld, the triumphs and tragedies of the divine tribe, and the delicate balance between mortal and magic. Through music, the Tuatha Dé Danann's story becomes a symphony that stirs the depths of the human spirit.

Beyond the realms of creative expression, the Tuatha Dé Danann's legacy continues to be celebrated through festivals, rituals, and gatherings. In the verdant landscapes of Ireland, people come together to honour and pay homage to the divine race, rekindling the ancient connections between the mortal and the magical. These celebrations, steeped in tradition and folklore, serve as reminders of the enduring enchantment that the Tuatha Dé Danann bestowed upon the land.

Archaeological discoveries, too, offer glimpses into the material remnants of the Tuatha Dé Danann's existence. The exploration of ancient sites reveals artifacts that bear the mark of their divine touch. Elaborate jewellery, intricately crafted weaponry, and ceremonial objects tell tales of a people whose skill and craftsmanship were matched only by their ethereal grace. These archaeological treasures provide tangible links to a past that remains alive in the collective memory.

"Enchanting Legacy: Unravelling the History of the Tuatha Dé Danann" concludes, but the story of this divine race is far from over. It lingers in the whispers of the wind, in the rustling of leaves, and in the hearts of those who are captivated by the allure of the magical and the mythical. The Tuatha Dé Danann, with their triumphs, their sorrows, and their eternal connection to the land, continue to inspire, to ignite the imagination, and to remind us that within the realms of myth, there lies a timeless wisdom and an eternal enchantment.

As you close this book, let the echoes of the Tuatha Dé Danann's story resonate within you. Carry their legacy with you and allow their presence to infuse your own journey through life. Embrace the magic that surrounds us, for in the spaces between reality and dreams, between the seen and the unseen, lies the eternal enchantment of the divine.

Steve McCarten - 2023

Chapter 1

Origins in Ancient Ireland

In the hallowed realm of ancient Ireland, where the veil between mortal and mystical grew thin, the stage was set for the arrival of a race that would etch their story into the very fabric of myth and legend. "Enchanting Legacy: Unraveling the History of the Tuatha Dé Danann" beckons us to tread upon the sacred soil of Emerald Isle, to immerse ourselves in the tales that spin a tapestry of origins for the illustrious race of the Tuatha Dé Danann.

Within the aged leather covers of this tome, the story unfolds like delicate strands of silver thread. It whispers of a time long past when gods and mortals walked hand in hand upon the verdant landscapes of the Emerald Isle. It is a tale of enchantment, of a race both divine and human, whose origins remain shrouded in mystery.

As we turn the brittle pages, the words come alive, dancing before our eyes like ethereal sprites. We are transported to a time when the land itself breathed with a magic so potent it could shape the destinies of nations. It is here that we encounter the Tuatha Dé Danann, a race of beings whose very existence was steeped in wonder.

Legend tells of their arrival on the shores of Ireland, descending from the heavens with a grace that defied mortal understanding. They were gods, it was said, possessed of otherworldly powers and a wisdom that surpassed all mortal comprehension. Their presence transformed the land, infusing it with a radiance that shimmered in every dewdrop and whispered in every breeze.

But their story is not one of unchallenged glory. For the Tuatha Dé Danann, like all beings of power, were not immune to the trials and tribulations of life. They were locked in an eternal struggle with the Fomorians, a race of monstrous beings who sought to usurp their dominion. The battles that ensued were titanic in scale, with the very earth trembling beneath the weight of their fury.

Yet, amidst the chaos and conflict, there were moments of breath-taking beauty. The Tuatha Dé Danann were skilled artisans and poets, and their works were imbued with a magic that transcended the mundane.

They crafted wondrous weapons and intricate jewellery, and their words could weave spells that would make the stars themselves weep.

The Tuatha Dé Danann were not just powerful warriors; they possessed a deep connection to nature and the mystical forces that flowed through the land. The hills and forests were alive with their presence, and the rivers and lakes sang with their melodies. They understood the language of animals and plants, and their songs could heal the sick and bring life to barren soil.

In their wisdom, the Tuatha Dé Danann recognized the delicate balance between the mortal realm and the realm of the divine. They knew that their time in Ireland was not meant to be everlasting, and they willingly made way for the arrival of humankind. They retreated into the hollow hills, the ancient mounds that became their mystical abodes. Yet, their influence continued to permeate the land, forever etched in the collective memory of the Irish people.

Through the ages, the stories of the Tuatha Dé Danann were passed down, whispered around hearth fires, and were woven into the very fabric of Irish culture. They became the stuff of legends, blending with the folklore of banshees and leprechauns, of faeries and giants. Their names echoed in the names of hills and rivers, in the ancient chants and incantations that were carried on the wind.

But in the modern world, where technology reigns and scepticism prevails, the Tuatha Dé Danann have become distant figures, fading into the mists of time. The enchantment they once embodied has been relegated to the realm of fantasy and imagination. Yet, the echoes of their presence can still be felt if one knows where to look.

In the quiet solitude of a moonlit glen, where the ancient trees whisper ancient secrets, one might catch a glimpse of their ethereal forms. In the shimmering waters of a secluded lake, where ripples form mysterious patterns, one might hear the faint echoes of their laughter. And in the hearts of those who carry the blood of Ireland, the spirit of the Tuatha Dé Danann continues to burn bright, an indelible mark that connects them to a legacy of magic and wonder.

"The Enchanting Legacy: Unravelling the History of the Tuatha Dé Danann" is not merely a book; it is a key to unlocking the hidden realms of imagination and possibility. It is a portal to a time when gods walked the earth and the boundaries between mortal and divine were blurred. Within its pages, we find ourselves journeying alongside the Tuatha Dé Danann, experiencing their triumphs and tragedies, their joys, and sorrows.

It is a tapestry woven with words, where the power of storytelling reveals its true potency. It reminds us that the myths and legends of old are not mere flights of fancy, but windows into the human psyche and the collective dreams of a culture. They hold within them the seeds of our own desires and aspirations, our longing for meaning and purpose.

As we delve deeper into the tapestry of their history, we begin to unravel the threads of their legacy. Their influence on Ireland was not simply one of power and might, but also of wisdom and enlightenment. They bestowed upon the mortal inhabitants of the land a gift of knowledge and inspiration, shaping the course of human civilization for centuries to come.

"The Enchanting Legacy: Unravelling the History of the Tuatha Dé Danann" is a testament to the enduring power of storytelling, to the way in which words can breathe life into long-forgotten tales and transport us to realms beyond our imagination. It invites us to embrace the magic that resides within us all, to see the world with wonder-filled eyes, and to honour the ancient bonds that connect us to the past.

As we close the book, we carry with us the echoes of the Tuatha Dé Danann, their stories etched upon our souls, reminding us that magic, in all its forms, still lingers in the world, waiting to be discovered once more. For within the depths of our own hearts, the ancient spirit of the divine still dances, whispering its secrets and urging us to embrace the enchantment that surrounds us.

Chapter 2

Arrival of the Divine Tribe

In the mystical tapestry of ancient Ireland, the threads of fate converged as the Tuatha Dé Danann set foot upon its verdant shores. Their arrival, heralded by whispers carried on the wind and the subtle shift of the land itself, marked a turning point in the history of the Emerald Isle. In the second chapter of "Enchanting Legacy: Unravelling the History of the Tuatha Dé Danann," we delve into the wondrous and captivating tale of their arrival, unveiling the secrets of their journey and the destiny that awaited them.

Legends, woven through the loom of time, recount the Tuatha Dé Danann's exile from a distant land, driven by forces beyond mortal comprehension. The waves embraced their vessels, carrying them across treacherous seas, guided by a celestial compass invisible to mortal eyes. With each passing day and each whispered prayer to the ancient gods, the shores of Ireland grew closer, their destiny entwined with the land they were bound to embrace.

Upon their arrival, the Tuatha Dé Danann encountered the Fir Bolg, the brave and resilient inhabitants of the island. This meeting of ancient tribes set the stage for a clash of power and destiny, a battle that would resonate through the ages. The Battle of Mag Tuired, a cataclysmic event etched in the annals of Irish mythology, unfolded with a fervour unmatched by mortal conflicts.

The chapter unfolds like a tapestry of cosmic forces intertwining. The Tuatha Dé Danann, their radiant forms illuminated by the light of the Otherworld, unleashed their supernatural abilities and strategic brilliance upon the battlefield. Spells of enchantment danced upon the air, weapons forged with celestial craftsmanship clashed, and the land itself trembled under the weight of their divine presence.

In this epic confrontation, the Tuatha Dé Danann emerged triumphant, solidifying their dominion over the land and displacing the Fir Bolg. It was a turning point, a seismic shift in the balance of power, as the divine tribe etched their destiny into the very fabric of the land. The defeated Fir Bolg, their stories and legacies intertwined with the Tuatha Dé Danann, would forever be remembered as part of the intricate tapestry of Irish mythology.

With their victory, the Tuatha Dé Danann sought to establish a seat of power that would embody their authority and connect the realms of mortals and the divine. The sacred hill of Tara, nestled in the heart of Ireland, became the very nexus of their dominion. Its slopes resonated with the energy of the land, while its summit stood as a beacon, a bridge between the earthly and ethereal realms.

At Tara, the Tuatha Dé Danann wove together the intricate threads of governance, spirituality, and ritual. Led by their noble and wise leaders, such as Nuada, the Silver-Armed King, and the mighty Dagda, they forged a society that flourished under the watchful gaze of the gods. It was a harmonious blend of artistry and mysticism, where the realms of mortal and divine intersected in an intoxicating dance.

The arrival of the Tuatha Dé Danann in Ireland was not merely a physical event but a convergence of cosmic forces, a symphony of fate and divine intervention. As they stepped onto the sacred soil, the land itself responded, its very essence resonating with their presence. The trees whispered ancient secrets, the rivers sang a melody of welcome, and the stones hummed with the energy of the Otherworld.

In their encounter with the Fir Bolg, a fierce and valiant tribe deeply rooted in the land, the Tuatha Dé Danann recognized both adversaries and kin. The clash of these ancient forces, like the clash of storm clouds in a tempestuous sky, was inevitable. The Battle of Mag Tuired became the crucible where destinies intertwined and the fate of Ireland hung in the balance.

With their mastery of magic and martial prowess, the Tuatha Dé Danann unleashed a symphony of power and enchantment upon the battlefield. Their weapons glimmered with ethereal light, their spells wove a tapestry of illusions and elemental forces. The very earth beneath their feet trembled with the echoes of their divine might. It was a clash of titans, a dance of gods and mortals, as the destiny of the land unfolded before the awe-struck eyes of those who bore witness.

In the end, the Tuatha Dé Danann emerged as the victors, their triumph etched into the annals of Irish mythology. The Fir Bolg, though displaced, would forever be remembered as an integral part of the intricate narrative of Ireland's ancient heritage. From this pivotal moment, the Tuatha Dé Danann established their reign and laid the foundations for a kingdom that would intertwine the mortal and the divine.

The sacred hill of Tara, where the power of the Tuatha Dé Danann would find its zenith, became a beacon of their authority and a testament to their connection with the land. At its summit, the High King of the Tuatha Dé Danann held court, presiding over matters of governance, justice, and sacred rituals.

Tara became a place of pilgrimage, drawing seekers of wisdom and solace from all corners of the land, for it was here that the divine and the earthly converged.

Under the wise and noble leadership of Nuada, the Silver-Armed King, and the benevolent guidance of the Dagda, the divine tribe flourished. They were not merely rulers but mentors, artisans, and guardians of the ancient wisdom that flowed through the land. Art and craftsmanship thrived under their patronage, their halls resounded with poetry and song, and their people revelled in a harmonious existence where mortal and divine coexisted in perfect balance.

Chapter 3

Divine Attributes and Enigmatic Powers

In the realm of the Tuatha Dé Danann, the boundaries of mortal limitations dissolved like morning mist. They possessed attributes and powers that surpassed the realm of ordinary existence, elevating them to a divine pantheon of beings beyond compare. In the third chapter of "Enchanting Legacy: Unravelling the History of the Tuatha Dé Danann," we embark on a wondrous exploration of their extraordinary gifts and magical prowess.

At the core of their essence resided an unparalleled mastery of magic. The Tuatha Dé Danann were the true sorcerers of the land, wielding ancient incantations and weaving spells that shaped the very fabric of reality. With words spoken in hushed whispers and gestures bathed in mystic gestures, they could call forth elemental forces, bend the laws of nature to their will, and traverse the boundaries between realms. They danced with the elements, conversed with the spirits, and commanded the unseen forces that pulsed through the world.

But their magical abilities extended far beyond the manipulation of the arcane. The Tuatha Dé Danann possessed an innate connection to the natural world, intertwining their beings with the pulse of life itself. They communed with animals, sharing their consciousness and assuming their forms. In the blink of an eye, they could become the soaring eagle, the graceful deer, or the cunning serpent. This shape-shifting power bestowed upon them the wisdom and instincts of the creatures they embodied.

Their enchantment was not limited to the realms of nature; it extended to the ethereal realm as well. The Tuatha Dé Danann, with their ethereal beauty, possessed an allure that stirred the hearts and captivated the gaze of mortals and immortals alike. Their luminous presence emanated from within, a radiance that transcended the physical form. It was as if they had taken fragments of starlight and wove them into their very being, drawing all eyes to their celestial glow.

Within the chapter, we unravel the tales that speak of their prowess in the realm of prophecy and foresight. The Tuatha Dé Danann boasted seers and oracles, individuals gifted with the ability to gaze into the tapestry of time, decipher its intricate patterns, and reveal the threads of destiny. Through their visions, they guided their people, shedding light on the path ahead and offering glimpses of what lay beyond the horizon. These mystics stood as bridges between the mortal realm and the ever-shifting currents of fate.

The Tuatha Dé Danann's creative brilliance was not confined solely to the realm of magic. Their skill in craftsmanship and the creation of enchanted artifacts was renowned throughout the land. Weapons, imbued with their divine essence, were crafted with meticulous care, each stroke of the hammer a testament to their mastery. The spear of Lugh, invincible and swift, became the embodiment of his warrior spirit. The cauldron of the Dagda, which never ran empty, symbolized abundance and nourishment. These artifacts were not mere objects; they carried the echoes of the Tuatha Dé Danann's power and became conduits of their enigmatic essence.

"Enchanting Legacy: Unravelling the History of the Tuatha Dé Danann" invites you to wander through the realms of wonder and mystery, to witness the manifestation of extraordinary gifts bestowed upon the divine tribe. Continue reading as we marvel at their mystical abilities, their ethereal beauty, and the enchanting artifacts that bore witness to their divine touch. Prepare to be captivated by the bewitching tapestry of the Tuatha Dé Danann, where the boundaries of possibility are stretched, and where the magic of their existence pulses in every breath.

Chapter 4

The Tuatha Dé Danann's Immortal Presence in Irish Mythology

In the ethereal tapestry of Irish folklore, the Tuatha Dé Danann stand as pillars of divine presence, the boundaries of mortal limitations dissolved like morning mist, their stories interwoven with the very essence of Irish mythology. In the fourth chapter of "Enchanting Legacy: Unravelling the History of the Tuatha Dé Danann," we embark on a mesmerizing journey through their profound influence on the rich tapestry of Irish lore, illuminating the paths they walked alongside the pantheon of gods and goddesses.

At the core of their essence resided an unparalleled mastery of magic. The Tuatha Dé Danann were the true sorcerers of the land, wielding ancient incantations and weaving spells that shaped the very fabric of reality. With words spoken in hushed whispers and gestures bathed in mystic gestures, they could call forth elemental forces, bend the laws of nature to their will, and traverse the boundaries between realms. They danced with the elements, conversed with the spirits, and commanded the unseen forces that pulsed through the world.

But their magical abilities extended far beyond the manipulation of the arcane. The Tuatha Dé Danann possessed an innate connection to the natural world, intertwining their beings with the pulse of life itself. They communed with animals, sharing their consciousness and assuming their forms. In the blink of an eye, they could become the soaring eagle, the graceful deer, or the cunning serpent. This shape-shifting power bestowed upon them the wisdom and instincts of the creatures they embodied.

Their enchantment was not limited to the realms of nature; it extended to the ethereal realm as well. The Tuatha Dé Danann, with their ethereal beauty, possessed an allure that stirred the hearts and captivated the gaze of mortals and immortals alike.

Their luminous presence emanated from within, a radiance that transcended the physical form. It was as if they had taken fragments of starlight and wove them into their very being, drawing all eyes to their celestial glow.

Within the chapter, we unravel the tales that speak of their prowess in the realm of prophecy and foresight. The Tuatha Dé Danann boasted seers and oracles, individuals gifted with the ability to gaze into the tapestry of time, decipher its intricate patterns, and reveal the threads of destiny. Through their visions, they guided their people, shedding light on the path ahead and offering glimpses of what lay beyond the horizon. These mystics stood as bridges between the mortal realm and the ever-shifting currents of fate.

The Tuatha Dé Danann's creative brilliance was not confined solely to the realm of magic. Their skill in craftsmanship and the creation of enchanted artifacts was renowned throughout the land. Weapons, imbued with their divine essence, were crafted with meticulous care, each stroke of the hammer a testament to their mastery. The spear of Lugh, invincible and swift, became the embodiment of his warrior spirit. The cauldron of the Dagda, which never ran empty, symbolized abundance and nourishment. These artifacts were not mere objects; they carried the echoes of the Tuatha Dé Danann's power and became conduits of their enigmatic essence.

Within the chapter's pages, the reader is invited to witness the awe-inspiring rituals through which the Tuatha Dé Danann channelled their magical abilities. In sacred groves hidden deep within the heart of ancient forests, they gathered under the moon's silver glow to commune with the spirits of the land. Their chants and incantations echoed through the night, blending with the rustling of leaves and the whispering of hidden streams. With every ritual, they reaffirmed their connection to the mystical forces that animated their world.

Their ceremonies were a delicate dance between the mortal and the divine, an intricate weaving of intention and reverence. They understood that true magic was born from a harmonious relationship with the natural world and a deep respect for the energies that pulsed through every living being. Through their rituals, the Tuatha Dé Danann sought not to dominate nature but to align themselves with its flow, to become conduits through which its power could manifest.

In the sacred groves, as the moonlight filtered through the canopy above, the Tuatha Dé Danann opened themselves to the whispers of the trees, the rustle of hidden creatures, and the sighs of the wind. They listened to the subtle harmonies of the earth, feeling the gentle thrum of life coursing through their veins.

In those moments, they were not separate from the world around them but integral parts of its tapestry, intricately woven into the grand design of creation.

As we immerse ourselves in their world, we come to realize that their powers were not just tools of manipulation and conquest but expressions of their intrinsic nature. The Tuatha Dé Danann embraced their magical gifts with reverence and responsibility, recognizing that true power lay not in dominion over others, but in the harmony, they achieved with the forces of creation. They were conduits of magic, guardians of the delicate balance between the mortal and divine, and custodians of the enchanting legacy that shaped the very fabric of their existence.

In the whispers of the wind and the rustling of leaves, we can still hear the echoes of the Tuatha Dé Danann's mystical chants, carried on the breath of time. Their enchantment lingers in the ancient hills and valleys, waiting to be awakened by those who seek to reconnect with the realms of magic and wonder.

Chapter 5

Battles and Conquests of the Divine Race

In the resounding echoes of history, the battles and conquests of the Tuatha Dé Danann reverberate through the ages, etching their indomitable spirit into the tapestry of their legacy. In the fifth chapter of "Enchanting Legacy: Unravelling the History of the Tuatha Dé Danann," we venture into the realms of epic conflicts and extraordinary triumphs that shaped the narrative of the divine race. With each battle fought and conquest achieved, the Tuatha Dé Danann showcased their prowess as formidable warriors and guardians of their kingdom.

This chapter unfurls with the legendary Battle of Mag Tuired, a monumental clash between the Tuatha Dé Danann and the Fir Bolg, whose echoes resounded throughout the annals of Irish mythology. The strategic brilliance and supernatural abilities of the Tuatha Dé Danann surged forth like a tempest, unleashing their might upon the battlefield. The winds howled with their wrath, the earth trembled beneath their feet, and the clash of weapons reverberated across the land. In this momentous conflict, the divine tribe emerged victorious, establishing their dominion over the land, and casting their influence upon the ancient Irish landscape.

The aftermath of the Battle of Mag Tuired brought forth a new era, a time of prosperity and enlightened governance under the rule of the Tuatha Dé Danann. Their reign was not one of mere dominance, but one marked by a deep connection to the land and its inhabitants. They viewed themselves as custodians, protectors of the natural world and patrons of the arts and knowledge. Their conquests had a profound impact on the fabric of society, as they established a harmonious relationship between mortals and the divine.

But their victories did not quell the storm of opposition. The Fomorians, ancient beings of chaos and darkness, emerged as a formidable adversary. These monstrous creatures, with their twisted forms and insatiable hunger for power, sought to overthrow the Tuatha Dé Danann and reclaim dominion over the land. Thus began a tumultuous series of battles, a relentless struggle between order and chaos, where the fate of Ireland hung in the balance.

The battles against the Fomorians were not only fought with weapons and brute strength but also with magic and cunning. The Tuatha Dé Danann employed their supernatural abilities to combat their adversaries, weaving spells and illusions that bewildered the Fomorian forces. They called upon the elements, commanding the winds to whip, the waves to rise, and the earth to quake. The very fabric of reality bent to their will as they unleashed their enchantments upon their foes.

In the midst of these conflicts, individual heroes emerged from the ranks of the Tuatha Dé Danann. Lugh, the shining champion, exemplified the blending of martial prowess and mystical talents. His spear, swift and true, struck down the enemies of his people. But his skills extended beyond the battlefield, for Lugh was also a Master of Arts and crafts, music and poetry. He embodied the multifaceted nature of the Tuatha Dé Danann, warriors and artists, magicians and philosophers.

Nuada, the Silver-Armed King, led his brethren with wisdom and grace. His silver arm, forged to replace the one he lost in battle, became a symbol of resilience and determination. With his strategic acumen and regal presence, Nuada guided the Tuatha Dé Danann through the trials of war, ensuring that their victories were not hollow but steps toward a better world.

And then there was the Morrigan, the enigmatic goddess of war, shrouded in mystery and ambiguity. She weaved her ethereal presence into the fabric of conflict, whispering courage into the hearts of warriors. She appeared as a crow, a harbinger of both doom and triumph, guiding the Tuatha Dé Danann through the darkest moments of their battles. The Morrigan, with her prophetic gifts and fierce determination, embodied the indomitable spirit of the divine race.

With each victory over the Fomorians, the Tuatha Dé Danann solidified their hold on Ireland and reshaped its destiny. Their rule brought forth an era of enlightenment, where the realms of mortals and the divine intertwined. They fostered a society that valued wisdom, creativity, and the preservation of the natural world. Under their guidance, the arts flourished, with songs and stories echoing their triumphs and trials through the ages.

But their conquests were not without their costs. The battles waged by the Tuatha Dé Danann took a toll on their warriors, both physically and emotionally. The scars of war ran deep, leaving indelible marks upon their souls. They carried the weight of loss and sacrifice, a reminder of the price paid for their victories.

"Enchanting Legacy: Unravelling the History of the Tuatha Dé Danann" invites you to delve deep into the battles and conquests of this mythical race, to witness their unwavering determination and their transcendence of mortal limitations.

Through the pages of this chapter, the echoes of their triumphs resound, their indomitable spirit etched into the very fabric of Irish mythology. It is a testament to their valour and the enduring legacy they left behind, a legacy that continues to inspire and captivate, reminding us of the power of myth and the extraordinary heights that the human spirit can attain.

As we immerse ourselves in their tales, we come to understand that their battles were not merely clashes of swords and spears, but profound metaphors for the eternal struggle between light and darkness, order and chaos. The Tuatha Dé Danann's triumphs symbolize the indomitable human spirit, the capacity to rise above adversity and create a better world. Their legacy transcends the realm of myth and speaks to the core of our collective consciousness, reminding us of the transformative power of courage, resilience, and the unwavering pursuit of truth and justice.

Through the ages, their stories have been told and retold, passed down from generation to generation, each telling adding new layers of meaning and interpretation. The battles and conquests of the Tuatha Dé Danann have become part of the cultural fabric of Ireland, shaping its identity and instilling a sense of pride and resilience in its people. They serve as a reminder that even in the face of seemingly insurmountable challenges, the human spirit can prevail and overcome.

"Enchanting Legacy: Unravelling the History of the Tuatha Dé Danann" is not just a book, but a portal to a world of magic, bravery, and the eternal struggle between light and darkness. It invites us to immerse ourselves in the rich tapestry of their battles and conquests, to witness the triumph of the divine race, and to reflect upon the profound lessons they impart. Through their stories, we are reminded that within each of us lies the potential for greatness, the capacity to rise above adversity and shape our own destinies. Their legacy lives on, their echoes resonating through the ages, inspiring us to embrace our own inner hero and embark on our own epic journeys.

Chapter 6

Bridging Realms: Divine Encounters and Mortal Alliances

In the ethereal realm where the divine and mortal intertwine, the Tuatha Dé Danann forged intricate connections that reverberated through the tapestry of Irish folklore. In the sixth chapter of "Enchanting Legacy: Unravelling the History of the Tuatha Dé Danann," we embark on a mesmerizing exploration of their interactions with mortals and other mythological beings, where the boundaries between worlds blurred and legends were born.

This chapter unravels the intricate tapestry of the Tuatha Dé Danann's relationship with mortals, a spectrum that spans from benevolent guidance to more complex entanglements. They assumed roles as mentors and patrons, their wisdom and protection sought by bards, warriors, and craftsmen alike. Mortals who displayed exceptional talent and virtue found themselves blessed by the divine tribe; their achievements elevated by the touch of otherworldly inspiration.

Among these mortals, the bards held a special place in the hearts of the Tuatha Dé Danann. They were the keepers of ancient tales, the weavers of words that carried the weight of history and the magic of the divine. The Tuatha Dé Danann showered them with their blessings, igniting the flames of inspiration within their souls. These chosen bards became vessels of the divine stories, their verses resonating with the power of the gods, their words carrying the essence of the ethereal realm to mortal ears.

But the divine race did not exist in isolation; they sought connections with mortals through marriages and alliances. These unions forged a bridge between realms, intertwining the divine and the human. Legendary figures emerged from these unions, individuals whose lineage blended the extraordinary qualities inherited from their divine heritage with mortal flesh and blood. The heroic figure Cú Chulainn stands as a testament to this divine-human lineage, a beacon of courage and prowess whose exploits surpassed mortal limitations.

Moreover, the chapter delves into the Tuatha Dé Danann's encounters with other mythological beings, expanding the horizon of their influence. Among these beings were the sídhe, the fairy folk who inhabited mystical mounds scattered across the Irish landscape.

The interactions between the Tuatha Dé Danann and the sídhe wove intricate tales of friendship, alliances, and, at times, conflicts, as the divine tribe navigated the complex web of mythological beings populating the realms of Irish folklore.

The Tuatha Dé Danann's interactions with the sídhe were marked by a delicate balance of cooperation and respect. They shared knowledge and secrets, exchanged gifts and favours, and at times, even intermingled their populations. These alliances forged bonds that transcended realms, shaping the very fabric of Irish folklore and inspiring generations to come.

But the tapestry of their encounters did not end with the sídhe alone. The divine race brushed shoulders with dragons, giants, and other supernatural entities that inhabited the ancient lands. These awe-inspiring encounters became the seeds of heroic quests and epic narratives, where mortal and divine converged in battles of strength and wits, revealing the boundless capabilities of the Tuatha Dé Danann as they traversed treacherous realms and overcame formidable adversaries.

The Tuatha Dé Danann's encounters with dragons were particularly emblematic of their divine prowess. These majestic creatures, with their scales shimmering like gemstones and their fiery breath, embodied the power of the supernatural. The Tuatha Dé Danann engaged in epic duels with dragons, their weapons clashing with the ancient beasts, and their magic intertwining with the draconic forces. These encounters became the stuff of legends, tales that echoed through the ages, inspiring awe and wonder.

Furthermore, the Tuatha Dé Danann's influence extended beyond the shores of Ireland, entwining with the mythologies of other Celtic lands.

In tales from Wales, Scotland, and Brittany, echoes of their divine presence resonated, forging connections, and mirroring their counterparts in distant lands. This interconnectedness broadened their reach, reinforcing their status as divine beings of widespread renown, their influence transcending the boundaries of individual lands to become an integral part of the wider Celtic mythos.

In their interactions with mortals and mythological beings, the Tuatha Dé Danann became enmeshed in a rich tapestry of stories that celebrated the complexities of the human condition. They bestowed their blessings upon mortals, guiding them on quests of self-discovery and offering glimpses into the realms beyond mortal understanding. But their relationships were not without conflict and tension, for the divine and the mortal are intertwined with a delicate balance.

Through the tales spun in this chapter, we come to appreciate the interconnectedness of the realms of myth and reality. The stories of the Tuatha Dé Danann and their interactions with mortals and mythological beings remind us that the boundaries between worlds are fluid and permeable, that the divine resides within us and around us, and that the magic of existence can be found in the most unexpected places.

"Enchanting Legacy: Unravelling the History of the Tuatha Dé Danann" invites us to immerse ourselves in the wondrous tapestry of Irish folklore, where the divine and the mortal dance in a delicate embrace. It beckons us to explore the intricate connections that span realms and generations, to discover the transformative power of encounters between the extraordinary and the ordinary. As we journey through this book, we are reminded that the legends of the Tuatha Dé Danann continue to shape our understanding of the world, inspiring us to embrace the magic and mystery that lie within and to weave our own stories into the ever-evolving tapestry of existence.

Chapter 7

The Fading Echoes of the Tuatha Dé Danann

In the ebbing twilight of time, the divine presence of the Tuatha Dé Danann began to wane, their ethereal radiance dimming as they retreated from the forefront of Irish mythology. In the seventh chapter of "Enchanting Legacy: Unraveling the History of the Tuatha Dé Danann," we embark on a poignant exploration of their decline and retreat from the mortal world, where the shifting tides of belief and the march of cultural change swept them into the realm of fading echoes.

This chapter delves into the gradual erosion of the Tuatha Dé Danann's influence, as a new wave of beliefs and cultural forces surged across Ireland, heralding the arrival of Christianity. The transformative power of Christianity reshaped the religious and cultural landscape, casting shadows upon the once-glorious prominence of the divine tribe.

As the radiant light of Christianity spread, the ancient deities and legends of the Tuatha Dé Danann found themselves assimilated or marginalized within the emerging Christian framework. Some of the figures of the divine race were reimagined as saints or merged with other Christian entities, their mythic narratives blending and merging with the new religious paradigm.

The chapter unravels the complex interplay between the old and the new, as the tales of the Tuatha Dé Danann, once fervently celebrated and passed down through generations, began to intertwine with Christian narratives. The stories of Lugh, the shining champion, and Brigid, the goddess of poetry and healing, became intertwined with the lives of Christian saints bearing the same names. The divine lineage of the Tuatha Dé Danann became enmeshed within the genealogies of Irish noble families, their bloodlines serving as a bridge between the pagan past and the Christian present.

With the assimilation of the Tuatha Dé Danann into the realm of Christian belief, their significance shifted, their roles transformed. They became part of a syncretic tapestry, where ancient and new traditions interwove, blurring the lines between pagan and Christian mythologies.

The divine tribe, once vibrant and revered in their own right became part of a larger narrative that sought to reconcile the old with the new, the pagan with the Christian.

Furthermore, the chapter delves into the concept of the Otherworld, the ethereal realm where the Tuatha Dé Danann sought solace. As Christianity gained ground, the divine tribe became synonymous with the mystical and elusive beings known as the Sidhe. The sacred mounds and sites associated with the Tuatha Dé Danann became gateways to the Otherworld, and the divine race was believed to retreat deeper into that realm, becoming enigmatic and elusive figures of folklore.

The fading presence of the Tuatha Dé Danann is explored with a sense of bittersweet longing, for their departure marked the loss of a vibrant and magical era. The chapter delves into the yearning for the old ways, the longing for a connection to the divine beings of old, even as Christianity became the dominant religious force. The echoes of the Tuatha Dé Danann's presence remained in the collective consciousness of the Irish people, lingering as a whisper of a forgotten time.

It is within the realm of folklore that the Tuatha Dé Danann found solace, their tales living on in the oral traditions of the Irish people. The chapter explores the ways in which the stories of the divine tribe endured, passed down from generation to generation, as a testament to their enduring legacy. The enchanting tales of Cú Chulainn's bravery, Brigid's healing touch, and the Morrigan's shapeshifting abilities persisted, carried by the words of storytellers who understood the importance of preserving the mythic past.

But even as the divine race faded from the forefront of Irish mythology, their legacy endured in the hearts and minds of the Irish people. The chapter delves into the remnants of their mythic tales, the echoes of their enchantment that lingered in the cultural traditions and folklore of the land. The artifacts they left behind, the tales woven in the tapestry of Irish heritage, ensured that the Tuatha Dé Danann would forever hold a cherished place in the collective consciousness of the Irish people.

As we navigate the delicate dance between fading myths and enduring legends, we are reminded of the impermanence of all things. The chapter serves as a poignant reflection on the ever-changing nature of belief, the shifting sands of cultural tides, and the profound impact of mythological beings on the human psyche. The Tuatha Dé Danann may have retreated into the realm of fading echoes, but their legacy remains, whispering through the ages, inviting us to ponder the mysteries of the divine and the enduring power of myth.

It is in the twilight of their presence that we find a profound appreciation for the tapestry of human belief and the evolving nature of cultural narratives. The chapter invites us to embrace the complexities of our cultural heritage, to acknowledge the interplay of old and new, and to recognize the power of myth to shape our understanding of the world. In the fading echoes of the Tuatha Dé Danann, we discover a reminder of the enduring quest for meaning and the profound impact of mythic tales in the human experience.

Chapter 8

The Legacy of the Tuatha Dé Danann in Modern Times

In the final chapter of "Enchanting Legacy: Unravelling the History of the Tuatha Dé Danann," we embark on a mesmerizing journey through the tapestry of time, where the divine race's legacy weaves itself into the fabric of modernity. Though the Tuatha Dé Danann's presence may have waned over the passing centuries, their influence and imprint upon Irish culture, mythology, and the collective imagination persist, casting an enchanting spell that transcends the boundaries of time.

This chapter delves into the cultural and artistic impact of the Tuatha Dé Danann, whose mythic narratives continue to inspire and ignite the creative flame. From the Celtic Revival movement that reignited interest in Celtic mythology to contemporary works in literature, poetry, and art, the divine tribe's legacy lives on, breathing life into the imagination of countless artists, writers, and storytellers. Their tales of epic battles, enchanting encounters, and extraordinary characters resonate with audiences, inviting them to immerse themselves in a world steeped in magic and myth.

The chapter unravels the intricate connections between the ancient tales and the artistic expressions of today. It explores how the enchantment of the Tuatha Dé Danann continues to inspire visual artists, who capture the essence of their ethereal beauty and otherworldly realms in vivid paintings, sculptures, and illustrations. The lyrical poetry and evocative prose of contemporary writers pay homage to the divine tribe, weaving their stories into the tapestry of modern literature. Their influence can also be seen in the realms of music and performance, as musicians and actors draw upon the ancient myths to create immersive and transformative experiences for their audiences.

Moreover, the chapter explores the enduring celebration and preservation of the Tuatha Dé Danann's heritage in modern times. Across Ireland, vibrant festivals, rituals, and gatherings pay homage to the divine race, ensuring that their stories remain alive and vibrant within the hearts of the people.

These celebrations serve as a bridge between the ancient and the contemporary, honouring the legacy of the Tuatha Dé Danann and fostering a profound connection to the ancient roots of Irish mythology. They are reminders of the everlasting power and enchantment that continues to captivate the imagination of the Irish people.

The preservation of the Tuatha Dé Danann's legacy extends beyond the realms of art and celebration. Archaeology plays a vital role in uncovering the physical traces of their existence. The chapter delves into the realm of archaeological discoveries, where the remnants of the divine race's presence stir echoes of the past. Through meticulous excavations of ancient sites, artifacts, and structures associated with the Tuatha Dé Danann, a deeper understanding of their material culture and the physical landscapes they once inhabited emerges. Each discovery unravels fragments of their history, painting a vivid picture of their existence and leaving traces for future generations to explore and contemplate.

Furthermore, the enduring fascination with the Tuatha Dé Danann among scholars, mythologists, and enthusiasts of Irish mythology is a testament to the divine race's everlasting allure. Their tales continue to ignite the flames of curiosity and spark intellectual discourse. Scholars delve into ancient texts, unravelling the intricacies of their mythology, while mythologists and enthusiasts explore the realms of interpretation and reinterpretation, breathing new life into age-old stories. The divine tribe's significance endures as a captivating subject of study and a wellspring of inspiration in the fields of folklore and Celtic studies.

In the closing pages of "Enchanting Legacy: Unravelling the History of the Tuatha Dé Danann," we are reminded that the divine race's influence reaches far beyond the confines of the ancient past. Their enchantment resonates through the ages, inspiring artists, scholars, and enthusiasts alike to delve into the depths of their mythic tales. The Tuatha Dé Danann may have retreated into the mists of time, but their legacy remains as a testament to the enduring power of myth and the eternal connection between the divine and the mortal.

It is worth noting the intriguing connection between the Tuatha Dé Danann and the rivers of Europe, particularly through the figure of Danu, the divine mother goddess. In Celtic mythology, Danu is often associated with rivers, representing the life-giving flow of water and the nurturing aspect of the feminine divine. The name Danu itself is believed to be derived from the Proto-Indo-European word for "river" or "flow." This association establishes a profound link between the Tuatha Dé Danann and the rivers that meander across the European landscape.

Danu's connection to rivers can be observed in various European mythologies, where similar figures are revered as goddesses of rivers and waterways. From the Danube in Central Europe to the Don in Russia, the echoes of Danu's influence can be traced along the course of these majestic rivers. The rivers themselves become channels through which the divine and mortal realms converge, carrying the essence of Danu's power and wisdom throughout the lands.

This connection to rivers highlights the interconnectedness of the Tuatha Dé Danann with the natural world and the elemental forces that shape it. They embody the harmonious relationship between humanity and the environment, reminding us of the sacredness of the natural world and the need to honour and protect it. The rivers become more than mere geographical features; they become symbols of the divine flow, guiding us towards a deeper understanding of our place in the grand tapestry of existence.

In conclusion, the final chapter of "Enchanting Legacy: Unravelling the History of the Tuatha Dé Danann" weaves together the threads of the divine race's enduring influence on art, culture, and scholarly exploration. It celebrates the ongoing resonance of their myths, the vibrant celebrations that honour their heritage, and the ongoing quest to unearth their archaeological traces. And amidst it all, the connection to rivers and the figure of Danu serves as a reminder of the deep-rooted bond between the divine and the natural world. The Tuatha Dé Danann's legacy lives on, inspiring and captivating the hearts and minds of those who seek to uncover the magic and mysteries woven into the very fabric of our collective consciousness.

Epilogue

The Eternal Enchantment of the Tuatha Dé Danann

As our journey through "Enchanting Legacy: Unravelling the History of the Tuatha Dé Danann" draws to a close, we are immersed in the timeless enchantment and eternal allure of this divine race. The story of the Tuatha Dé Danann transcends the confines of mortal existence, weaving its way into the very fabric of the cultural tapestry, where its echoes resonate in the hearts of people, not just in Ireland but across the world.

Their legacy, like an unbroken melody, weaves its way through the generations, whispering secrets of ancient power and wisdom. The tales of their battles, their magic, and their profound interactions with mortals continue to captivate the imaginations of young and old alike, carrying the ancient flame of their divine essence from one era to the next. The Tuatha Dé Danann stand as guardians of the timeless human spirit, their stories symbolizing resilience, wisdom, and the enduring power of the human imagination.

Their influence reaches far beyond the realms of myth and legend. The Tuatha Dé Danann have become archetypes of the eternal bond between humanity and the natural world. They embody the intrinsic harmony between mortals and the divine, reminding us of the delicate balance we must maintain, the reverence we must hold for the Earth, and the preservation of ancient wisdom amidst the ever-shifting tides of modernity.

"Enchanting Legacy: Unravelling the History of the Tuatha Dé Danann" beckons you to continue your exploration of their mythology, to peer into the depths of the mysteries surrounding their origins, their triumphs, and their graceful retreat. Their story is a testament to the enduring power of storytelling, the resilience of ancient traditions, and the profound impact of myth on the human experience.

As you gently close the book, remember that the enchantment of the Tuatha Dé Danann extends far beyond its pages. It resonates in the whispers of the wind, in the murmurs of ancient landscapes, and in the quiet recesses of your heart.

Their tale serves as a reminder that even amidst the ebb and flow of the ever-changing world, the echoes of the divine persist, beckoning us to uncover the extraordinary within ourselves.

May the legacy of the Tuatha Dé Danann continue to ignite the spark of wonder, to kindle the fires of imagination, and to guide us on our own journeys through the realms of dreams and infinite possibilities. Embrace the enchantment that lingers in their wake, and allow their story to intertwine with your own, for it is through the melodies of their ancient song that we find the enduring magic that lies within us all.

ABOUT THE AUTHOR

Steve is an Irish author and filmmaker with a passion for ancient Irish folklore and mythology. Born and raised in Belfast, he developed an early fascination with the stories and legends that surrounded him, inspiring him to delve deeper into the rich cultural heritage of his homeland.

With a degree in Psychology and a love for storytelling in both written and visual domains, Steve has spent his career spanning several years as a marketing specialist before bringing his focus back to the myths and legends of ancient Ireland.

His most recent focus is writing a screenplay about the heroic tales of Airmid, Goddess of Healing and Rebirth of the Tuatha Dé Danann.

Made in United States
Troutdale, OR
09/29/2024